WHAT THEY SAY ABOUT ~~~
HOLMES B
" one of the ı
Sherlock Holn

" one of the world's
(THE Bı

AND FROM READERS...

"...good pastiches of the Sherlock stories are hard to come by. I think Mr. Ashton does an extraordinary job of making me feel like this could have been part of the original Canon."

" For those who love Sherlock Holmes, you will love these pastiches by Hugh Ashton. Engaging and written in Conan Doyle's style."

" 'The game is afoot' lives on in the writings of Hugh Ashton. If Sherlock Holmes has intrigued you in the past, gather together around the dispatch box of John H. Watson series. Get them all and dig into a welcome return to Sherlock and his cases."

" The last products of the Dispatch Box once owned by John Watson, M.D. are superbly crafted, including two stories that Dr. Watson transcribed from Holmes' notes and turned into a story of some worth."

" There is a consistency of voice and the stories ring true to the originals. Ashton has become one of the best writers of Sherlock Holmes stories, and if you are a fan, this is a must."

" When trying to emulate Doyle, Hugh Ashton is at the top of the list."

The Adventure of the Bloody Steps – Featuring the celebrated consulting detective, Mr. Sherlock Holmes

Hugh Ashton

ISBN-10: 1-91-260562-7
ISBN-13: 978-1-912605-62-0

Published by j-views Publishing, 2019

www.HughAshtonBooks.com

www.j-views.biz

publish@j-views.biz

j-views Publishing, 26 Lombard Street, Lichfield, WS13 6DR, UK

THE ADVENTURE OF
THE BLOODY STEPS

Colophon

W E DECIDED that this adventure of Sherlock Holmes deserved to be reproduced on paper in as authentic a fashion as was possible given modern desktop publishing and print-on-demand technology.

Accordingly, after consulting the reproductions of the original Holmes adventures as printed in *The Strand Magazine*, we decided to use the TT Barrels font as the body (11pt on 13.2). Though it would probably look better letterpressed than printed using a lithographic or laser method, it still manages to convey the feel of the original. The flowers are Bodoni Ornaments, which have a little more of a 19th-century appearance than some of the alternatives.

Chapter titles are in Amarante, and page headers and footers are in Baskerville (what else can one use for a Holmes story ?), and the decorative drop caps are in Romantique, which preserves the feel of the *Strand*'s original drop caps.

The punctuation is carried out according to the rules apparently followed by the Strand's typesetters. These include double spacing after full stops (periods), spaces after opening quotation marks, and spaces on either side of punctuation such as question marks, exclamation marks and semi-colons.

This seems to allow the type to breathe more easily, especially in long spoken and quoted exchanges, and we have therefore adopted this style here.

Some of the orthography has also been deliberately changed to match the original – for instance, " Baker Street" has become " Baker-street" throughout.

The Adventure of
THE BLOODY STEPS

HUGH ASHTON

 views

J-VIEWS PUBLISHING

LICHFIELD, ENGLAND

EDITOR'S NOTE

HERLOCK HOLMES rarely ventured out of the surroundings of London. Occasionally he visited the West Country, and only once or twice visited the Midlands or the North, at least as far as the documents available to us show.

However, it transpires that there were a few cases which Watson felt were worth his time recording, but for one reason or another failed to find their way into the collections published in Holmes' lifetime, and some of these take Holmes out of his usual geographical haunts.

This story, untitled by Watson, but which I have entitled "The Adventure of the Bloody Steps" is set in Rugeley, a small town less than ten miles from where I am writing this. The story of the unfortunate Christina Collins, who was viciously raped and murdered by drunken bargees in 1839, forms a background to this adventure, which is vaguely referred to in "The Bruce Partington Plans", when Holmes says, "Suppose that I were Brooks or Woodhouse, or any of the fifty men who have good reason for taking my life...". However, it is hard to see why the villain here should seek such extreme revenge on Holmes, as disappointed as he might be at the disruptions to his personal life and to his professional criminal career.

As to why Watson (or maybe Holmes) chose to suppress this, I can offer two possible explanations. Firstly, there is the Victorian prudishness and delicacy regarding homosexuality, which is hinted at here, though never explicitly spelled out. Secondly, there would have been a perceived slight to the Established Church had the facts of this case been made public. Though Holmes (and possibly Watson also) can hardly be described as committed Christian believers, my opinion is that they felt that the reputation of the Church of England, as a part of the Establishment, must be upheld.

Whatever the reasoning, Holmes here displays his skills in a manner that would do justice to any of the publicly recorded cases.

It is to be noted that Watson attempts to reproduce some of the accent and dialect used in this part of the world at the time. My feeling is that he was unsuccessful in this regard, and that the true South Staffordshire dialect of those days was different, almost to the point of unintelligibility to a Londoner. However, I have not attempted to "translate" his words, and have reproduced them as he wrote them.

Lichfield
April 2019

ARELY in my experience did one of Sherlock Holmes' cases start in such a way that gave no clue as to its unexpected and dramatic conclusion. It began with a letter addressed to Holmes at Baker-street, which arrived with the morning post one morning in 188–.

After opening the envelope and scanning its contents, he tossed it and the letter onto the table with an expression of disgust.

" Pah! These constant requests for investigation of matters that more properly pertain to the profession of fabulist than detective will be the ruin of me," he exclaimed.

" Why? What is it?" I enquired.

" See for yourself, and tell me what you make of it," he invited me. " Pay no attention to the contents at present, but simply tell me what you see in the letter and envelope themselves."

I picked up the envelope and letter and started to examine them, employing such of Holmes' own methods as I could. " The postmark is from Rugeley, a town with which I am personally unfamiliar, although the name has some resonance," I started. " The address has been written in a hand which appears to be of one unaccustomed to writing, which differs from the educated hand in which the letter has been written, though the pen and ink appear to be the same. There is a large dirty fingerprint on the back of the envelope, which was presumably imprinted when the envelope was sealed."

" Excellent as far as it goes, Watson, though you have omitted the most important points. Rugeley is a coal-mining town in Staffordshire, as can be confirmed by the particles of coal-dust adhering to the thumbprint – not made by a finger, incidentally, as you will admit if you take the trouble to examine it a little more closely. The reason that the name may be familiar to you is that Rugeley was the town from which the infamous poisoner, Palmer, hailed. He was hanged in 1856, following a trial at the Old Bailey. The aforementioned thumb was used to spread the glue that was used to seal the envelope, and the print, carrying the grains of dust, actually appeared before the envelope was sealed. The thumb, by the way, bears the marks of two cuts or scars which have yet to heal, indicating that the man – for this is undoubtedly the thumbprint of a man – is engaged in a manual occupation, maybe as a miner.

" As you rightly remark, the handwriting of the envelope and the letter differ. The envelope was addressed, we may assume, by the man who provided us with the thumbprint and who sealed the letter, and consigned it to the postal services. The letter on the other hand..." Holmes took the letter back from me, and scrutinised it with one of his lenses, bringing it close to his face before handing it back to me. " Ah, yes. A left-handed female writer. Educated, as you say, quite probably privately, by a French governess."

" How can you say such things ? " I asked, astonished.

" The left-handedness is elementary. The sex of the writer is easily deduced from the aroma of lilies of the valley emanating from the paper."

" And the French governess ? "

" The shape of the 'a' and 'f' closely resembles the way in which our Gallic cousins are taught to represent them. It is, of course, not impossible that the writer is herself French, but the quality of the language used in the letter would seem to preclude that as a possibility. Read it to me, if you would."

I started to read. " ' St. C____ Rectory, Rugeley, Staffs.'

Dated yesterday. 'Dear Mr. Holmes, I feel I must turn to you as my ONLY hope. Once more there is BLOOD upon the Bloody Steps, and poor Christina Collins has been seen once more. My husband, the Reverend Ezekiel Thornby, REFUSES to believe what I have seen WITH MY OWN EYES, and which has been witnessed by MANY OTHERS, and will not allow me or anyone to report this to the police. I URGENTLY require your assistance, and your assurance that I am NOT MAD, and that there is something that threatens us all from beyond the grave. Yours, Anna Thornby, (Mrs.).'" I put down the letter. "What does all this mean? Who is Christina Collins, and what are these Bloody Steps? Yet another message from a lunatic, I fear, Holmes."

"Certainly the work of a disturbed mind. And yet she possessed the wit to write to me, and to have another address and post the letter, thereby evading her husband's scrutiny. If this be lunacy, it is of an uncommon intelligence. As to the Bloody Steps and Christina Collins, I have an inkling that I have heard of this in the past. Have the goodness to pass me the volume by Beardson entitled 'Notorious Crimes in the Midlands of England'. I fancy you will find it on the second shelf to the right of the fireplace, between Norton's 'Fishes of the North Sea' and Holtzen's 'Beobachtungen über Kohlenteer-Derivate'".

I discovered the work in the place that Holmes had described and passed it to him. He flicked through the pages rapidly until he reached the point for he was searching. "Hah! This is it. In 1839 a young woman, Christina Collins by name, was travelling as a passenger on a canal barge to London. Somewhere close to Rugeley, the bargees, who had been paying her unwelcome attentions throughout the course of the journey, were found to have assaulted and killed her, throwing her body into the canal. They were tried and hanged in Stafford."

" And these 'Bloody Steps' ? "

" The body was found near a flight of steps which lead down from the road to the canal, which is raised above the Trent valley at that point and crosses via an aqueduct. It was said that the blood from the body stained the steps when it was carried up them, and no matter how many times the steps were cleansed of the blood, it would always re-appear."

" It seems to be a common superstition when it is a question of old castles and the like," I commented, " but it is interesting that it has survived into this modern age."

" True. I wonder," Holmes mused, " whether we should visit Mrs. Anna Thornby and investigate the matter ? "

" I see no reason to do so,"I objected. " Why should you concern yourself with the fancies of a hysterical woman living in a provincial town ? "

" There is something here that intrigues me," Holmes answered slowly. " I cannot at present put my finger upon it, but beneath the hysteria, there may well be a seed of common-sense and reality. The fact that these visions have been seen by others may well prove to be the divide between imagination and reality. At present, I will not inform Mrs. Thornby of our movements, if for no other reason other than preventing further discord and dissension between husband and wife."

For my part, I suspected Holmes of seeing himself as being under-employed, and regarding this trip as a diversion which would yield little, if anything, of importance or interest. Nonetheless, I packed my Gladstone with the basic necessities, and on a whim, added my medical bag to my baggage. We set off from Euston, and alighted at

Rugeley Trent Valley station where, after a little difficulty, we secured transport to the Talbot Inn, which Holmes informed me had formed the venue for the inquest on the unfortunate Christina Collins.

The evening meal we were served was passable, but the beer, hailing as it did from nearby Burton upon Trent, was excellent. I attempted to follow the conversations of the others drinking at the bar, but found it impossible to follow the heavy accents.

" It is a difficult turn of phrase for outsiders," commented Holmes. " I fear we are less than welcome here."

Indeed, this seemed to be the case. Some of our fellow-drinkers were casting suspicious looks in our direction, and I had no doubt that they were more than somewhat curious as to our reasons for being in Rugeley. One of the fellows made his way over to us, and asked us roughly what we thought we were doing.

" Why, we are here to find out more about the Bloody Steps and the woman who was killed there. We're writing a story for one of the London newspapers," Holmes said easily. " Would you know anything about this story? "

" Not me," said the man, " but Jim over there'll tell you more. It was his granddad, so he says, who carried the poor lass up those steps. London, eh? " He seemed impressed by the mention of the capital, but it was noticeable that there was no deference in his words to us or in the manner of his speech – factors that marked almost all of those with whom we conversed in this town of independent-minded individuals .

The man whom he indicated came over to join us, and Holmes offered to buy another round of drinks for the whole party, an offer which was readily accepted.

" Your health," said ' Jim', raising his glass to my friend.

"Aye, it was my father's father who helped lay the poor lass to rest. And he walked across the Chase to Stafford to see them boatmen hang. She's in the churchyard now, you know. Some of the folk here took pity on her and took up a subscription to give her a decent burial and a stone."

"Not that that put her to rest," said the first man. "You tell them what your granddad told you, Jim."

Jim took a look around the room and dropped his voice before continuing. "What he told me was that she kept coming back to the Steps after her killers was hanged. Many folk saw her just standing there. And the blood that dropped on the steps when my granddad and the others carried her – why, it never went away. They tried cleaning it, scrubbing it, but nowt worked. The blood was still there, and it would stay there till Doomsday, that's what they said."

"And is it still there?" Holmes said. It was the first man who answered.

"Now, it's funny you should be asking that. It's been quite a few years since Christina Collins was seen by the steps, and since the blood was seen on them, but for the past month or more—"

"Going on for three months now, Jack," Jim interrupted.

"More like two," Jack countered. "Anyhows, there's been blood on the Steps, so they say, and there's been the figure of a woman seen at the top."

"And have either of you two seen anything?" Holmes asked.

Both men shook their heads. "Haven't been up that way for some time. Now, the rector's wife, she's a strange one anyway, but she was one of the first who said that she'd seen something, according to my missus, who heard it from the cook at the rectory."

" How did she come to be there? The rector's wife, I mean. 'Tain't as if it's on the way to anywhere," asked Jim.

" I'm only telling you what my missus told me was told her by Betty. She said that Mrs. Thornby had been taking some soup or summat to old Lydia Yardley, that being Betty's husband's aunt, and was coming back the short way to the rectory when she saw this figure at the top of the steps. A woman's figure, she said, and she couldn't see the face, but she could make out that it was probably a young woman by the way she held herself."

" And then? "

" She called out to her, but there was no answer, and according to Betty, Mrs. Thornby could see through her. I mean, she could see the trees and all through her. And then she vanished, so she said."

" Interesting, to say the least," Holmes remarked. " Has anyone else seen this apparition? "

" Just a load of women, and you know how daft they can be at times. They say so, but I dinna believe them. But then there's the blood."

" Ah." Holmes sat forward in his chair. " Tell me more."

" Well, Betty said that Mrs. Thornby felt the steps go slippy-like when she went down them back home, running away from the ghost or whatever it was she thought she saw. The next morning she told Arthur Machin, who does the rectory garden, and he went to look. There was blood there, sure enough."

" Not red paint? " Holmes enquired.

" Arthur Machin knows blood right enough. He's slaughtered enough pigs in his time to know what he's talking about."

" And the blood is still there? "

" So they say. Haven't been there myself."

"We should be going there tomorrow," Holmes announced. "Another glass of beer, gentlemen?"

Despite Holmes' best efforts, it seemed that there was little more to be learned from these men, but, as I could not help remarking to Holmes as we mounted the stairs to our room that all seemed to be based on hearsay.

"Indeed so," he answered me, "but there is hardly ever some smoke without a fire underneath it."

"But surely," I protested, "there can be no such thing as a ghost, and the story of the blood is too preposterous to be believed."

Holmes smiled. "I am sure that Mrs. Thornby is completely sincere in her belief of what she has seen. As to exactly what she has experienced, we will discover more on the morrow."

The next morning saw us walking up the path to the front door of the rectory, following a wretched breakfast at the inn. As we neared the house, I was surprised to see the angry face of a man gesticulating at us through the window of one of the front rooms. Suddenly, the face vanished, and a few seconds later the door burst open to reveal a red-faced middle-aged portly man in clerical dress.

"Be off with you!" he shouted at us. "I want none of your sort here. My wife is not to be disturbed. Now go, before I call for the police to remove you!"

"An invitation it would seem churlish to ignore or refuse," remarked Holmes, as we turned and retraced our steps to the gate that took us onto the road. "Let us make our way to the famous Steps. I obtained directions from mine host this morning."

However, we had not gone a few yards before we were accosted by a giant of a man, whose black beard framed a friendly smile. "You'll have been to the Reverend's, then?"

I nodded agreement.

" He's none too friendly these days, since his wife saw Christina Collins and the blood on the Steps."

" And why would that be?" asked Holmes.

"Well, he's a queer one, the Reverend. He doesn't seem to understand us at all. Well, I suppose that's not too unusual with them Church folk, especially one like that who only came here just over a year ago. Most round here are Chapel, anyway, like me. But he does like to keep himself to himself. Now take me, I'm the gardener there, and —"

" Ah, you are Mr. Arthur Machin, then?" Holmes asked.

"You'll have got my name from Jim last night, then? I met him this morning, and he told me about you two. Newspaper gents from London, come to see the Steps."

" We were just on our way there," I explained.

" Then I'll take tha. Maybe I can tell a few things tha's not heard."

Machin told us more grisly details of the original crime that had led to the blood on the steps, as he had heard them as a boy from his uncle. It appeared that the unfortunate young woman had been on her way from the North to meet her betrothed in London, and had unaccountably decided on transport by canal barge as her means of transport. The bargees at that time were considered to be a wild and lawless section of society, and some claimed to have heard a woman's cries from the barge as it passed through locks a little to the north of the town. She had even complained to agents of the company that owned the barge, and to lock-keepers about the language of the boatmen, and the unwelcome attentions they had shown to her.

There was little doubt in anyone's mind, it was said, that the bargees had violated the poor woman, and killed her.

" And these latest doings ? "

" Well, that's a funny one, to be sure. The Reverend Thornby is a strange one, like I said. Hardly goes out of the house, unless it's to take services in his church, though some say they've seen him out late at night doing God knows what. Not that I've seen that, anyway."

"And his wife ? "

" Now she's a poppet, she is. Married the Reverend six months ago, but they didn't have the wedding here. Somewhere down south in her town, I heard. Pretty as a picture is that one, and sweet-tempered with it. Not two things tha sees together that often, I reckon." Holmes nodded in response. " It was her what took me on as the rectory gardener only a week or two after she came here, which I do for her when there's not so much work down the pit, and I have to say I couldn't be working for a better mistress. Always a please and a thank-you, and there's never any trouble about money."

" And was it you who posted a letter to London for her the other day ? "

Machin started. " Why, yes it was. Bist tha the gent she wrote to ? Mr. Sherlock Holmes ? "

" That is myself," Holmes acknowledged.

" I've read of tha in the papers, then. Tha's the one what solves those mysteries where the police can't manage it themselves."

" That is one way of putting it," Holmes smiled.

" Aye, she wrote a letter, but she didn't have an envelope to put it in without asking himself, and she didn't want him to know that she was sending it, so she gave me the letter and an address and the money for the stamp and an envelope."

" I see," said Holmes. " I had deduced that it was something along those lines, but it is always gratifying to have one's conjectures confirmed. And did you read the letter?"

The other was indignant. " No, I did not. I know better than to read a lady's private letters."

" But did she tell you what it was about?"

" She did that. It was all about the Steps, which we're just coming to, here on the right, and what she had seen there. The Reverend said to her that she was going mad when she told him about what she had seen, and she didn't want him to know she was writing to you."

" Would you say that she was frightened of her husband, then? Is he a violent man?"

" Violent with his fists, you mean? No, not that. But he has a temper on him, that one. He's not one you'd want to cross."

" We saw something of it just now."

We had reached a point in the pathway where a flight of worn stone steps led upwards. They appeared to be covered with some dark stains.

" This is the blood?" Holmes asked. Without waiting for an answer, he bent to examine it more closely.

" Aye, it's blood right enough," Machin said.

" I agree. But human blood?"

" That I couldn't say."

" Nor I," confessed Holmes. " Now, did Mrs. Thornby tell you what she had seen?"

" Aye. It was a figure of a woman, but it was dark, so she couldn't see the face. Just there, she said to me that it was," he added, pointing to a spot on the bank. " She called out, but there was no answer. And what really worried her was that she could see through it, she said. You see that farmhouse over there?" and he indicated a building some half a mile distant. " She said the lights was on there, and she could see the lights through the figure."

" And then?"

" She ran back to the rectory."

" Natural enough in the circumstances, I would have said. And then?"

" She told me her husband had gone out to visit the workhouse. The only person in the rectory was the man they keeps to look after the horses and some of the work around the house, Tom Leighton. She told me that she told him what she had seen, and he laughed at her."

Holmes shook his head. " Tut, tut. Most distressing. What manner of this man is this Leighton?"

" He's not from around these parts. He's from somewhere south of here. Keeps himself to himself most of the time, and we never see him in the Talbot or anywhere. Just doing some of the marketing. Women's work," he added in a tone of some disgust.

" They don't employ a maid for that?"

" No. Mrs. Thornby has a maid, but that's what they call a lady's maid, who just looks after herself, and don't do that much around the house. Janet came with Mrs. Thornby. Pert little thing she is, though she must be forty if she's a day. And then there's Betty Malpas who cooks for them. And then there's Tom Leighton, who calls himself Thomas because Tom's not grand enough for him, I reckon, does some of the things that maids do, like the marketing. He worked with Mr. Thornby before he was married, they say, as some kind of secretary, but he does other things around the house as well."

" And what manner of man is he?"

The other laughed. " Some would hardly describe him as a man. All dolled up in fancy clothes and with his hair just so, even though he's meant to be taking care of the horses and such. Not a man's man, if you take my meaning."

" Most interesting," Holmes answered. " His age and appearance?"

" He's not that young," was the answer, after some thought. " Perhaps thirty or thereabouts. Not a tall man, perhaps a little shorter than your friend there," indicating me, " and thin as a waif with it." He picked at his thumbnail for a few seconds, and looked up. " What's tha thoughts on the ghost, then?" Machin demanded.

" I have never seen a ghost," Holmes answered, " but I know those who have claimed to do so. However, on further investigation, I have come across little in the way of evidence to support those claims.

Machin appeared to consider this for a moment. " What about this here blood, then?" he asked Holmes. " That's real enough, ain't it? Tha can't deny that, can tha?"

" I certainly agree that it appears to be blood, but there is no way for me to determine whether it is human blood or not. It could be pig's blood, for example."

At these last words, Machin started. " Tha's not saying I did it, is tha?" he exclaimed, with a tone of menace in his voice.

" My dear fellow," Holmes replied easily. " Why in the world would I ever suggest such a thing? It is true that I remember one of your friends in the public bar last night telling us that you have some experience in slaughtering pigs—"

" That's true enough," replied the other. " I've been doing that since I was a lad of thirteen."

" —but that is hardly a sufficient cause for me to accuse you of playing a trick like that," Holmes continued, as if Machin had not spoken. "After all, you have expressed a warm regard for Mrs. Thornby. It would hardly seem consistent that you would attempt to frighten her with such a childish trick."

Holmes' words appeared to mollify the Midlander, who sullenly nodded his head. "Well, them's the Bloody Steps," he told us, "and you must agree that they have been named right."

"Indeed so," I agreed. I waited for him to leave us, as he seemed anxious to do so, but still remained near us. However, it was soon borne upon me that he was waiting for some sort of financial reward for his actions as a guide, and I pressed a florin into his hand.

"Why, ta," he said, with an air of simulated surprise and what seemed to be a slightly ironic air. "That's most generous of you."

Out of the corner of my eye, I could see Holmes was amused by this exchange. Again, it might be that one who was unacquainted with his moods might be unaware of this, but to my practiced eye, it was unmistakable. As Machin made his way back up the steps to the footpath leading to the Wolseley road, Holmes' face broke into a broad grin.

"Well done, Watson," he said to me. "Now we can examine all of this in a little more detail with no further interruptions." His attention seemed to be focussed on a thorn bush at the bottom of the steps. He examined it carefully, and using a pair of forceps, took something from a twig, and placed it in one of the envelopes he habitually carried with him for occasions such as this. He bent to examine the ground, and again picked up some almost invisible object which he placed in another envelope.

" It is fortunate that it has rained quite recently, making the ground soft and amenable to footprints," he remarked. " Maybe the trifles I have just observed will be of some use."

" Then you believe that Mrs. Thornby saw something? " I asked.

" Indeed I do, but I am positive that there was nothing in the least supernatural about what she saw." He walked to the steps. " And now for the blood." He pulled a small wooden spatula from his pocket and used it to probe the stains on the stone steps, peering at the result through his lens.

" See for yourself, Watson," he invited me. " It is evident that the blood has been applied on more than one occasion. There are several layers here which are clearly visible."

I took the lens and indeed, it seemed that there were several layers of the dark red stain, indicating that the liquid had been applied at different times.

" What do you think might be the object of this? " I asked.

" It is reasonably clear to me that the blood, and the 'ghost' that have been seen here are intended as deterrents to prevent investigation of this area. Something is amiss here, and I have my suspicions that the answer lies in the rectory."

" Why on earth should you suspect anything to be amiss there? "

" I have my reasons," he answered, with a shrug. " Come, I have seen all I need to see at present. Let us make our way up the Bloody Steps."

As we approached the rectory, we could see in front of us the figure of what appeared to be Thornby, the rector, walking away from us in the direction of the town.

"Excellent," commented Holmes. "We may yet meet Mrs. Thornby, and this mysterious Leighton while the ill-tempered rector is away."

We walked along the road, when I suddenly stopped.

"What is this?" I asked, bending to pick up a glove that was lying by the side of the road. "Someone will be sorry to have lost this." It was a dark kid man's glove, and it hung strangely from my fingers before I passed it to Holmes, who placed it in his coat pocket before we walked on. We entered the rectory garden, and rang the front bell, which was answered by a young man, who from his appearance could be none other than Leighton, who had been described to us earlier. His manner and general clean-shaven appearance could best be described as "unmanly", and his voice when he spoke was one which would not have seemed unduly out of character if it had issued from a woman's mouth.

On our enquiring after Mrs. Thornby, he regretted, with many polite evasions and flourishes, that she was currently engaged in some charitable errand in the town, and she had not informed him when she would be returning.

"Who shall I say has called on her?" he asked us.

Holmes dismissed the question with a negligent wave of his hand, instead withdrawing from his pocket the glove that I had observed him pick up earlier. "Does this belong to anyone here?" he asked, extending the object before him, explaining that we had found it by the side of the road only a few minutes earlier.

The effect on the other was surprising. His pale face drained of whatever colour it had previously possessed, and he stammered as he declared it to be his property. Holmes handed it to him, a faint smile on his face.

We made our farewells, and turned back towards the road, Holmes chuckling quietly to himself. "Well, at least we know the identity of our ghost, do we not?"

"You mean that young milksop?" I asked. "Why, you have hardly set eyes on him," I exclaimed, "and yet you are already accusing him of complicity in some nefarious scheme."

"Complicity indeed, but he is not the guiding spirit, of that I am sure." He chuckled quietly. "However, it is possible that he may be acting as a spirit of some kind."

"I can hardly guess at your meaning," I answered.

"Come, Watson, you do not believe that the spirit of the poor girl who died some fifty or more years ago continues to haunt this place, do you?"

"With so many witnesses, there must be some truth to the story, surely."

"Indeed there probably is some truth. But why do you believe that it must have some sort of supernatural explanation? This world is strange enough without us bringing the next world in to fill the gaps in our understanding."

"Then you believe that someone is impersonating the ghost? Leighton?"

"Precisely."

"And he is spreading blood, maybe pig's blood, using the story of these Bloody Steps for some purpose of his own?"

"Exactly."

We walked on in silence, when we were accosted by a man whom I recognised as having been one of our conversational partners in the public house the previous evening.

"I didn't want to say anything back there last night," he

told us, jerking his thumb backwards in the direction of the hostelry where we had talked. " But there's summat funny going on with that Arthur Machin," referring to the gardener of whom we had so recently taken our leave.

" And what might that be ? " asked Holmes.

" Well, I was telling you last night that he slaughters pigs. It's one of the ways he makes his living, along with the gardening and such like, and he does it for all the folk around here. Now, what he does is to save the blood to make black puddings, and Arthur Machin, well, he's a generous sort of man, and he just gives this blood away to anyone who asks him for it. Well, my missus went round to his house just the other day to ask him for some of the blood, and he told her that he didn't have any. Now that was queer, because he'd killed Bill Stubbins' pig just the day before, and he wouldn't have used all that blood in one day, would he now ? "

" I lack your experience in these matters," said Holmes, but I am sure you are correct. Did he give a reason to your good lady for the absence of the blood ? "

" No, he did not."

" And your conclusion ? "

" Well, I don't like to speak ill of a man like Arthur who I grew up with since I was a lad, but I reckon he's the one putting the blood on the steps, like."

" It is a theory that certainly has something to recommend it," my friend answered gravely. " What about the ghost that some claim to have seen ? "

" Now that's not going to be Arthur Machin, is it now ? " replied our informant.

" Why do you say that ? "

" Well, he's a big man, isn't he ? There's no-one in this town who'd ever mistake him for a young lass, even in the dark. Mind you, there's one round these parts who you might take for a girl."

"You are referring to Thomas Leighton?"

"Aye. You've met the b____, then? You'd agree that he'd make a fine figure of a woman?"

"There is definitely something in what you say," Holmes agreed.

"I'll be leaving you with that thought," our interlocutor said to us before turning away.

"Our friend has just stumbled upon the truth, has he not?" Holmes remarked as we walked towards the town. "Leighton does indeed make a perfect substitute for the shade of Miss Collins, does he not? In the dark, with the right draperies, I am sure that he achieves a fine imper- sonation of a ghost."

"To what end?"

"Ah, it would be premature of me to reveal my thoughts as of now, while they remain as mere suspicions. We must investigate a little further. But halloa! I feel that we are about to meet Mrs. Thornby."

Indeed, a lady was approaching us, whose dress and general demeanour seemed to be other than that of the usual local inhabitants of the place.

As she drew near, Holmes tipped his hat to her, and ad- dressed her as " Mrs. Thornby".

"You have the advantage of me, sir," she replied, clearly startled by Holmes' words.

"I am Sherlock Holmes," he explained, "and this is my friend and colleague, Doctor Watson," indicating me.

She gave a little start of surprise. "I do not remem- ber that you informed me that you would be visiting this Godforsaken place."

"In what way can you level that charge at the town,

madam?" Holmes asked her. "Your husband is in charge of what appears to be a fine church, and we have spoken to your gardener, Mr. Machin, who seems to be a regular attender at Chapel, from what I could gather. Surely the Almighty has not entirely deserted this place?"

She smiled thinly. "After my previous life in rural Hampshire, I am afraid that this is hardly a desirable location for me. But may I invite you to come into the rectory? The street is hardly a suitable place to hold this conversation, I feel."

"I am afraid that your husband was somewhat emphatic in his expression of his wish that we leave, telling us that you were not to be disturbed."

She smiled, but there was little humour in her expression. "Indeed I have been greatly disturbed by what I have experienced here lately, and I hardly think that your presence will inconvenience me more. In any event, my husband has gone to Lichfield for the day. Allow me to invite you to our home."

We turned towards the rectory for the second time that day, and were conducted to a room which presumably did duty as a sitting-room, meagrely furnished. Mrs. Thornby rang a bell, and requested the maid to bring us tea.

"I must apologise," our hostess told us, "for the state of the place. A parson's stipend is not great, and I have not been long enough here to furnish the place to my liking."

"You are recently arrived, here, I take it?"

"Not six months ago," she agreed. "I came here following my marriage to Mr. Thornby, not knowing precisely what to expect. Though I admit that the people here are kind enough in their way, this is not a place I would choose to live of my own volition."

"May I ask how you met your husband?"

She paused. "You may consider me a foolish woman, but to tell you the truth I hardly knew my husband when I married him. I am not as young as my appearance might suggest to you, and I had a horror of being left on the shelf, as the saying has it.

"He visited my parents' village for a week's holiday, and paid his attentions to me. I was naturally flattered, and when he proposed marriage to me, I accepted, without being fully aware of what this might entail.

"I suppose that most would term him a good husband, but oh, this place..." Her voice trailed off before she resumed her speech. "The town is filthy with coal dust, I can hardly understand what the people are saying, and there is no society here worthy of the name. And then, to add to all this, there is the apparition of the Bloody Steps."

"May I ask you about that?"

"Of course. This was my original reason for inviting you here, was it not?" Holmes nodded, and she continued, "I had been visiting one of my husband's parishioners, a Miss Yardley, taking her some hot soup, and I decided to take the path by the canal—" Here she made a gesture in the direction of the place from which we had come. Holmes assured her that we had been there ourselves, and we were familiar with the location.

"Very well, then," she continued. "It was dusk, and I was approaching the steps – that is to say, the ones that they term the "Bloody Steps" – I saw a slight figure standing at the foot of the steps. It was dressed in a black cloak or some sort of wrapper. Though the face was partly obscured by the cloth, a breeze blew the cloth aside, and the face was revealed briefly."

"A woman's face?"

"It was visible for only a short time, and the light was dim, but yes, I believed it to be a woman's face."

"And what led you to believe that the figure you saw was in some way supernatural?"

"Mr. Holmes, I do not consider myself to be unduly imaginative, or in any way, but I had an impression of pure evil when I saw that face. Furthermore..." She paused, and Holmes invited her to continue. "Furthermore, it was my distinct impression that the figure was – how shall I say this? – transparent. I distinctly remember seeing the steps and the bushes through the figure. I turned away, perhaps to see if there was anyone there who would be able to confirm what I believed I was witnessing, but there was no-one. And when I turned back, the figure was gone."

"Did you approach the place where you had observed the figure?"

"I confess that I was too frightened to do so. I stood, rooted to the spot, for what seemed an eternity, but in truth was probably no more than a minute. When I examined the place where I had seen the figure, there was no trace of anyone's having been there."

"And then?"

"I raced up the steps to the rectory. When I entered, I called out to my husband, but he was not present. His secretary, Leighton, was there, and I told him what had occurred."

"His reaction?"

"I am sorry to say that he simply laughed at me, and regarded my tale as a foolish woman's fancy."

"Indeed, most distressing," I commented.

"Upon his scornful dismissal of my fears, I took myself to my room, and told the tale to my maid, who was more sympathetic than Leighton. She administered some sal volatile and I recovered myself somewhat. When my husband returned from his duties, I told him all that had passed, but he refused to credit my words, and brusquely informed me that I must have been mistaken."

Holmes' next question to Mrs. Thornby came as a surprise to me. "What did Machin have to say to you when he heard about this?" he asked.

"Why, I never told him anything, but my maid Janet talked to our cook, Betty Malpas, and she must have been gossiping with her, and that is how the story will have reached Machin's ears.

"I met him the day after I had seen the— whatever it was that I did see that night, and he was kind enough to tell me the grisly story of the poor young woman who was assaulted and murdered there. I may add that he is one of the members of this community who shows the most kindness and friendliness towards me, though he is not a regular worshipper at my husband's church. I had never heard it before, which makes it more unusual that I saw the figure of a young woman, not knowing the history of the place."

"Indeed," agreed Holmes. "And the blood on the steps?"

"I had never noticed it before, to tell the truth. It was dark when I saw the figure, and it was impossible to distinguish any details. The only detail I can add is that it felt slippery under my feet."

"I see," commented Holmes. "May I turn to another subject, that of Thomas Leighton?"

She made a slight *moue* of disgust. "If you must, though I hardly see what he has to do with this matter."

"It is my habit to gather as much information as possible on the circumstances and the people surrounding an incident. It is impossible to ascertain at the start of an investigation exactly which matters will prove trivial, and which vital. What can you tell me about him?"

" He acts, as I am sure you have been informed, as secretary to my husband, though I hardly feel that the demands of the parish here justify such a position. He also does some other work around the house, such as would be expected of a female domestic, which may be considered an eccentricity on my husband's part to employ him in this way. Although, as I have mentioned, the stipend here is far from generous, it is my husband rather than the Church who is responsible for his board and keep, and his salary. He had joined my husband's employment here a little time before our marriage, though he behaves with a familiarity that would suggest a longer association."

" I see. And your feelings towards him?"

She leaned forward and lowered her voice to an almost inaudible level. " There is something about him that makes my flash creep. He is, in a word that we used as girls at school, 'sneaky'. One never knows where he will be, listening at doors, or peering through windows. To be frank with you, Mr. Holmes, I detest the man. "

As she concluded her speech, Holmes rose from his chair and silently made his way to the door, putting his finger to his lips. With no warning of what he was about to do, he flung open the door to reveal Leighton on the other side, bending down, seemingly having had his ear applied to the keyhole.

" I... I was simply retrieving a handkerchief which I had dropped," stammered the secretary, and indeed, there was a square of white cloth in his hand. He appeared to recognise Holmes and myself, and started. " What are you doing here?" he demanded of us, but Holmes remained silent. "I swear to you that I heard nothing," he protested.

"Why, no-one was accusing you of anything," said Holmes, smiling at him. "However, to avoid any such suspicions in the future, I would strongly recommend that you take yourself away from here." We watched Leighton remove himself and move down the passageway, and Holmes closed the door. "I begin to understand your problem," he said to Mrs. Thornby. "And I believe that it has a material, not a supernatural, cause. With your permission, we will leave you now, and I trust I will be able to supply you with a satisfactory explanation of the situation within twenty-four hours. For now, I can assure you that your imagination is not playing tricks – though I have a strong suspicion that there are tricks being played of a very corporeal nature."

"Why, thank you, Mr. Holmes," said our hostess. "You have already relieved my mind immeasurably. My one fear is that the Leighton creature will inform my husband of your presence here, and that he will become angry with me."

Holmes' face took on a look of concern. "You fear your husband's anger?" he asked.

"He dare not strike me," she answered. "He knows full well that my money and property are mine and mine alone, and I have the power to deprive him of their use."

Holmes and I resumed our seats. "This would seem to add a new angle to the problem," he commented. "You have not said so in so many words, but you would appear to imply that your husband married you primarily on account of your money."

She bowed her head. "I did not want to say this, but I fear it to be the case. As I say, I was impetuous in my affection for him, and perhaps I failed to perceive his true motives in marrying me."

"Would you describe him as an affectionate spouse?" I asked her.

"Hardly that, I fear. Indeed, you might well describe me as a neglected wife. I have attempted – oh, how I have tried – to be a good rector's wife. I visit the sick, I attend the services and offices at which he officiates. I provide him with as comfortable a home as our circumstances allow, but still I wait in vain for a sign of his affection. Why, I believe that he thinks more of that Thomas Leighton creature than he does of me." She buried her face in her hands, and appeared to be weeping silently.

"My dear Mrs. Thornby," I said to her, rising, and placing a hand on her shoulder. "You must be strong, and place your faith in Sherlock Holmes here. If there is one man in England who can unravel the problems that you currently face, it is he."

She raised her face to me with a look of gratitude. "It is good of you to say so, Doctor Watson."

"In the meantime," I continued, "you may find this cordial to be of value in settling your nerves." I reached in my bag for a bottle that I handed to her. "Three drops in a glass of water to be taken after meals."

She received it from my hand with a suitable word of thanks, and we rose once more to leave the house.

Once we had left the premises, Holmes turned to me. "I trust that the sedative you gave to her will have no adverse effects."

I laughed. "I will be most surprised if it does," I answered him. It consists of a little vinegar, and some caramel dissolved in water. I find it to be most efficacious with women who are undergoing emotional upheaval, such as Mrs. Thornby is suffering at present."

"Excellent, Watson. Your oath to do no harm is obviously well observed in this case. Now," rubbing his hands together, "tell me what we have learned today from Mrs. Thornby, when we combine it with the information we have received from other sources."

"We appear to be dealing with a marriage of convenience," I answered. "She complains of a lack of attention to herself, while the Leighton creature, as she terms him, appears to occupy a closer place in her husband's affections. I do not wish to make assumptions here, but—"

"Quite so," Holmes cut me off short. "Let us not turn our speculations in that direction. We can assume, however, that Thornby and Leighton were acquainted with each other prior to the former's removal to this town, can we not? Our next task is to discover where they might have met, and under what circumstances. I wonder," he continued, "if there might be a library in this town, with a copy of *Crockford's*?"

We enquired of a passer-by and were informed that the Free Jubilee Library was situated in Bow-street. It proved to be relatively well-stocked, and after hearing Holmes' request, the librarian directed us to the shelves where the clerical directory was located.

Holmes turned the pages, and with a grunt of surprise, looked at me. "Watson, how old would you guess the Reverend Thornby to be, based on our brief meeting earlier?"

"I would not put him above forty years of age?" I answered.

"Not sixty-eight?" Holmes asked, smilingly.

"By no means," I retorted.

"See here," my friend told me, pointing to an entry in the book. I looked, and beheld the name of the Reverend Thornby, and a date which would indeed make him sixty-eight years old.

"There is more than one Reverend Thornby?" I suggested, but Holmes shook his head.

"There is but one."

"Then the man in the rectory is not the Reverend Thornby, it is clear. Who is he, then?"

"I believe his name to be William Brooks."

I was taken aback by this assertion. "How in the world can you say that? Do you know the man?"

"It is true that we have never met face to face," Holmes answered me. "On the other hand, I it may be that I know a great deal about this man whom we met so briefly earlier. If I am correct in my suspicions, and I fully believe that I am, he is one who has proved most successful in his profession, which is that of 'fence', or one who disposes of stolen goods. I had my eye on him two years ago, but he suddenly dropped out of sight, and I was unable to determine where he had gone. Obviously he took on this new identity, and moved himself here, where there were few checks made on his antecedents."

"It seems incredible that he should be able to pass himself off as a clergyman," I said. "Could a common criminal such as he convince a congregation that he was an ordained minister of the Church?"

"Not as difficult for him as it might be for some," Holmes said to me. "He has had the advantage of a University education, though he never took his degree, being sent down for a series of petty thefts from his fellow-students, according to my sources."

"I can scarcely credit it. But how do you come to

suspect this Brooks of this impersonation? And what is his purpose here?"

"One question at a time, my dear Watson," Holmes admonished me. "As to his identity, that hinges on the glove that we discovered in the road, and passed to Leighton at the rectory. I must send a telegram to Hopkins at the Yard. His answer will conform my suspicions. Come, to the post-office."

Holmes sent his reply-paid wire, with the answer to be delivered to the Talbot, where we repaired to await the answer, and to take our midday meal.

As we sat over the roast pork that mine host had provided for us, the pig from which it was taken probably having been slaughtered by Machin I asked Holmes about his further conclusions regarding the ghost that Mrs. Thornby claimed to have seen.

"I do not deny that she must have seen something. She appears to me to be a sensible woman, unlikely to imagine something entirely. However, I do consider that her imagination has caused her to misinterpret various natural phenomena." Here Holmes reached in his pocket, and extracted an envelope, which I recognised as one which he had used to store something that he had picked up from the Bloody Steps. "What do you make of this?" he asked me, laying the scrap of cloth before us on the table.

I examined the item as minutely as possible under the circumstances, but was unable to provide any answer, other than to reply that it seemed to be a piece of dark gauze.

"Precisely, Watson," was Holmes' reply to me. "At times it would appear to be a solid cloak, but in the flickering gloom of the evening, it would at times appear to be transparent. Hence, Mrs. Thornby would perceive it at times as being a solid figure, and at other times as a ghost."

" And the feminine face ? What woman would play such a trick ? "

" It was no woman that Mrs. Thornby saw," Holmes said meaningfully. " As you know, we have encountered the 'ghost' twice today already, and I expect to have further dealings with him again before the day is out. See here." Upon his saying this, he extracted the second envelope from his pocket, and placed the object that he had removed from the steps on his plate. " See here," he invited me, passing his high-powered lens.

I looked, but could see little. " I see a seed-like object embedded there, but I fear I do not recognise it."

" It is a seed of the tree *Araucaria araucana*, commonly known as the monkey-puzzle tree."

" Is there anything strange about it ? The area is surrounded by trees."

" Indeed so, but there were no trees of that genus to be seen in the area. Indeed, there is only one such tree that I have observed in this town. It is in the rectory garden."

" Is it not possible that Mrs. Thornby unwittingly carried it from the garden and deposited it there ? I cannot see this seed as proof of anything."

" I would agree with your conclusion, Watson, were it not for the fact that the seed was partially embedded in the dried blood coating the step, thereby implying that it was dropped there when the blood was still in a liquid state, probably by the man who spread the pig's blood on the steps."

" Arthur Machin ! " I exclaimed. " He is the rectory gardener, and he is the one man in this town who seems to have access to the pig's blood and the tree."

"Why do you not assume that the man who impersonated the ghost is also the one who spread the blood?"

"I do not consider it likely," I told my friend. "Leighton seems to me to be too much of a milksop to engage in some such practices.

Holmes said nothing in reply, but merely smiled, and re-applied himself to his food. We had nearly finished our meal, when the landlord approached us, bearing a telegram, which he handed to Holmes, who tore it open with a grunt of satisfaction.

"Excellent!" he commented. "I have always maintained that Hopkins is, together with Gregson, one of the rising young stars in the firmament that is Scotland Yard. He has risen to the occasion admirably. Here, read this."

He passed the telegram to me and I read the following, "BROOKS LEFT HAND TWO SMALLEST FINGERS MISSING." I paused. "I understand the meaning of this, but who is William Brooks, and what is he to us here?"

"Ah, there I believe my professional knowledge puts me at an advantage over you. As I was saying to you earlier, William Brooks is well enough known in his trade, which is that of 'fence', or receiver of stolen goods. Perhaps I should say that he was well-known, as he disappeared from sight somewhat above eighteen months ago.

"Now, it is important not to draw conclusions before all the facts are known, but since Brooks' disappearance, within this last year, there have been several robberies recently in provincial cities, where the purloined items have been offered for sale in London a matter of weeks later, all through the same agency."

"Then the police have simply ignored this?"

Holmes shook his head. "Naturally, they have questioned the owner of the shop where the articles were for sale, but were unable to prove that the purchase was anything other than legal, even though the items were indisputably those which had been stolen in Manchester, Liverpool and Birmingham. All attempts to locate the supposed vendor of the items have failed, invariably leading to a false address. Without further proof, the police have been unable to act."

"If I remember correctly, the Reverend Thornby has been rector here for just over a year, according to what we read in the library."

"Indeed."

"But pray, why did you ask Hopkins about the missing fingers?"

"Because Leighton has all his fingers still."

"I fail to understand you."

"You remember the glove that we picked up in the road and we presented to Leighton?"

"Naturally."

"Was it a left-handed or a right-handed glove?"

"I cannot remember."

"It is these little matters, Watson, that may send a man to the gallows, or allow him to prove his innocence and walk away from the dock as a free man. In this case it was a left-hand glove, made by Mercer's of London. Also, as you may have noticed, the two smallest fingers of the glove were packed with cotton-wool, such as might be used to disguise the fact that the wearer was missing those fingers from his hand.

"When we presented Leighton with the glove, I took care to examine his left hand, and it transpired that none of his fingers were missing. There is, to our knowledge, only one other adult male in the household, Thornby, so I concluded that the glove was his. This deduction was also partially confirmed by the confusion displayed by Leighton on receipt of the article."

I turned over these facts in my mind. " And the connection with Brooks ? "

" I had heard it mentioned that Brooks was missing some fingers, but I had not heard which fingers, or on which hand. The story is that he lost them as the result of a bloody dispute with an Amsterdam jeweller over the price of some diamonds that he was attempting to sell. I knew that he had been arrested in the past, and that Scotland Yard would have a record of his physical characteristics, including any missing fingers, and I therefore telegraphed Hopkins to obtain that information."

" I believe I am beginning to see the plan," I said. " Somehow, as you suggested earlier, this Brooks has taken on the identity of a genuine priest who was appointed as rector here, in order to carry out some nefarious scheme. Where is that priest who was appointed here ? "

Holmes shook his head. " I fear the worst. Brooks and his operations are, I believe, controlled by a man who sits in the centre of the criminal life of this country like a spider in his web, pulling a thread here and spinning another trap there. He and his organisation will stop at nothing to achieve their foul ends. I fear that the murder of a priest would mean little or nothing to them. I have yet to make my final reckoning with this man, but I believe that our paths will collide sooner or later."

" Surely," I objected, " those making the appointment of the rector would have noticed some discrepancy between the man who presented himself as Thornby, and the man whose description we read in *Crockford's* ? "

" It is quite possible that this is not the case," Holmes said. " According to what we read, the Reverend Thornby was previously the incumbent of a remote parish in Northumberland. It is extremely unlikely that anyone here would have personal knowledge of the man. In any case, it is a simple matter to add or subtract a decade or two from one's age. I have done it myself, you may recall, with some success."

" But why should Brooks choose to make his home here, of all places ? " I asked. " And who is Leighton ? "

" As to the first, consider," my friend said to me, " the location of this town, and its nature. We have here a station on a direct line which takes us to the south directly to London and to the north to Crewe, and hence to Manchester and Liverpool. We also have a line into Birmingham, and some of the major towns to the north of that city. It is not too far from the Great North Road or from Watling Street, which passes close to Lichfield, less than ten miles from here. Consider also the canal which we have just visited. From there, it would be a simple matter to transfer the proceeds of a robbery, for example, from any part of the country to any other part."

" One would hardly suspect this small Midlands town to be the nexus of the traffic in the country's criminal proceeds, but I can well believe it now that you make the case. And you believe this to be so ? "

" Stanley Hopkins was kind enough to lay the little problem regarding the proceeds of the robberies that I mentioned earlier before me, and I was of the opinion that there existed a central point at which the goods were collected, and then sent on. Little did I suspect, however, that in coming here I would discover this to be the central point.

"As to the second question, there have been rumours concerning a certain indelicacy associated with Brooks' private life. I have little doubt that Leighton, or whatever his true name may be, along with whatever other moral failings he may possess, has links to the criminal organisation to which I alluded just now, and acted as Leighton's accomplice in the past, prior to their removal to this place."

" I guess we may take it that Thornby, or Brooks, as I suppose we must term him, took a wife on account of her money and her property?"

" Of that, I am sure. The marriage would also provide a cover of respectability for his operations. An unmarried man living alone with one such as Leighton, would be certain to set tongues wagging in the town."

" The purpose of the ghost and the blood on the steps was to deter visitors to the place?"

" Of course. It is almost certain that the proceeds of the burglaries were transported by canal to this place, prior to distribution to other parts of the country, or to ports. For example, diamonds could easily be sent to Amsterdam for disposal."

" A truly ingenious scheme. Who would ever dream of searching canal barges for stolen goods?"

" Who indeed? Their lack of speed would actually prove an advantage in this capacity. By the time they reached this place from their point of departure, the hue and cry would have died down."

" And the booty would be taken to the rectory, and stored there before being passed on?"

" We may assume so. Again, a perfect hiding place. What police agent would dream of searching the home of a man of the cloth for jewellery purloined from a house some seventy miles distant?"

"And what are we to do? We have no warrant for his arrest or to search the house."

"We must wait by the Bloody Steps tonight and take our chances. There was a robbery in Sutton Coldfield not a few nights ago which bears all the hallmarks of the others. It is quite likely that the proceeds have been transferred to a nearby canal and will be making their way to this point, either tonight or in the next few days."

"And Machin's part in all this?"

"Machin is implicated, to be sure. But I do not consider him to be guilty. My belief is that the blood was stolen from him, and that he might have had his suspicions as to the guilty party, he was unwilling to make a definite accusation without more definite proof. You may have remarked some bloody footprints at the Steps, which can only have been left when the blood was still in liquid form, meaning that they were the prints of the person who had spread the blood?"

"I did notice them."

"When we were talking to Machin, I took the liberty of directing him, without his being aware of the fact, to a soft patch of ground. While you were rewarding him for his services as a guide, I examined the prints that he left there, and compared them with the footprints on the Steps. It is impossible that he is the one who left those prints, meaning that it was another who was responsible for the blood."

"Then how is he implicated if he is not responsible for the blood on the steps?"

"I am sure that the blood came from his stores, and he knows it, even if he did not give permission for it to be removed. Surely you must have noticed his unease when we

talked to him, and his genuine concern for Mrs. Thornby's
welfare."

"Very well, then, I am your man. At what time should
we begin our vigil?"

"A little before it turns to dusk, which at this time of
year is about seven o'clock."

Accordingly, we waited at the inn until that hour,
Holmes being of the opinion that there was little to be
done until that time, and we set off once more for the
Steps. Holmes had, with his customary foresight, located a suitable hiding-place for us on our previous visit, and
we concealed ourselves, none too comfortably, behind a
thick bush through which it was still possible to observe
the canal.

We had waited for perhaps an hour in the gathering
gloom before a horse-drawn barge appeared, and was
moored by the bank. The horse was turned loose from
the boat, though still tethered, and immediately began to
graze on the rich grass of the bank by the tow-path.

I felt Holmes nudge me in the side with his elbow, and
looked in the direction in which he was pointing. A dark
shadowy figure had appeared on the Steps, and though I
knew it to be Leighton clad in a cloak of dark gauze, I re-
alised how Mrs. Thornby had believed that she was able to
see through the figure. The slight breeze ruffled the cloth,
and my hair stood on end, as I perceived the bushes behind the figure through it.

Leighton, for it was certainly he, made his way slowly
down the Steps, and I could now discern another more
solid figure at the top.

"It is Brooks," whispered Holmes almost inaudibly.
"He is waiting for the 'ghost' to disperse any onlookers."

Leighton slowly approached the barge, with an almost

gliding gait, with his impersonation of a supernatural spirit calculated to inspire fear in any observer.

One of the bargees, who had been lounging in the stern of the boat, smoking a pipe, addressed Leighton, but the words were unintelligible at this distance, being spoken in a dialect that was unknown to either Holmes or myself.

Leighton replied, and again we were unable to make out the words, but the boatman stood up, holding in his outstretched hand a small bag.

Leighton took it, and after opening it and apparently examining the contents, reached in his pocket and pulled out what appeared to be an envelope, which he handed to the boatman.

"It is time!" Holmes said to me, and sprang from our place of concealment with a wild shout. I followed him, adding my own version of a Pathan war-yell to his cries.

As we approached Leighton, the barge's horse, seemingly startled by our noise, appeared to panic, and moved rapidly away. In its haste, it kicked up its hooves, striking Leighton on the head and sending him, seemingly senseless, into the water.

The bargee who had received the money from Leighton instantly threw a rope towards him, but it appeared that the unfortunate man was in no state even to recognise that assistance was being offered, let alone to take advantage of it.

I made as if to strip off my coat and enter the water to save the drowning man, but Holmes restrained me.

"Leave him be," he instructed me. "It will save the cost of a rope and a hangman's fee."

I was somewhat shocked by the callous nature of these words, but could appreciate their sense, and refrained from further action.

A wild cry came from above us. "Thomas!" wailed Brooks. "Will no-one save him?" He rushed down the steps, and stopped short when he recognised Holmes and myself.

"What are you doing here?" he demanded, but did not wait for an answer, rushing to the waterside. "Save him!" he demanded, pointing at the floating body. "I cannot swim. It is you who must rescue him. For God's sake!"

Holmes stood impassively, still gripping my arm, and restraining me, against all my instincts, from saving the life of a fellow human being, no matter how foul his character.

Having done what he obviously saw as being his whole duty, the boatman sat back, relit his pipe, and placidly regarded the sight of Leighton's body floating in the water.

"You ____!" screamed Brooks at the impassive bargee, letting forth a string of invective which I will not bother recording here. "And you!" indicating Holmes and myself. Without warning, he reached inside his coat and pulled out a revolver. "Take that, you ____!" he screamed, loosing off all six chambers in our general direction, though fortunately, his shots all went wild, missing us by several feet at least. The sound of the gun startled the horse, which bolted, tearing out the stake which had tethered it, and it went cantering along to tow-path. At the same time, the rooks roosting in the trees were awakened by the noise, and soared into the sky, their hoarse cries almost deafening us.

With a snarl of rage, Brooks hurled the revolver towards us in apparent disgust before fleeing up the Steps at a run.

"And that, I fancy," commented Holmes, "is the last we or anyone will see of the Reverend Thornby. I will wager that we discover his clerical clothing discarded in a ditch on the way to the station. Naturally, the Yard will continue to keep a sharp lookout for William Brooks. And as for you, my lad," turning to the stupefied boatman, " I think you had better come with us to the police."

" You can't make me come with you," objected the other.

" Very true," admitted Holmes. " However, we do have the name of your boat, and a watch may easily be set up and down the waterways of England. And without a horse, I do not think you will be travelling very far."

" All right," agreed the bargee. " But I've done nothing. You wait till I tell them."

He shouted to someone inside the boat, and a woman emerged. " I'll be back soon," he informed her. " The horse has gone off again. Best get Jem or Lizzy to go after her." With that, he stepped onto the shore and took up a position between Holmes and me.

" What was in the bag you passed to him ? " Holmes asked him as we set off up the steps.

" God's truth, I don't know. That bag was sealed, and I was told it was more than my life was worth to open it. All I knew was that I had to deliver it to that nancy-boy who you saw just now and I'd get paid. No one told me about any b____ parson coming along, firing a b__ great gun at me, though."

" How much did they offer you ? "

" Twenty pounds is what they told me. I'm hoping that they got it right."

Holmes let out a low whistle. " Good pay for a few minutes' work," he said.

" That's what I thought to myself when they asked me," the boatman told us.

" How many times have you done this, then ? " Holmes asked him.

" That's the first time, honest."

"And it will be the last, I am sure," Holmes commented, grim-faced.

At the police-station, Holmes explained the facts of the matter to the sergeant on duty, who promised to keep an eye open for Brooks, and dispatched two of his men to the Steps to recover Leighton's body.

"Though if what you say is true, sir, the Reverend, or whoever he might be, is on his way to London or beyond by now, and there's not a lot we can do about it."

The boatman continued to protest his innocence, but upon opening the envelope which he believed to contain the twenty pounds he had been promised, it was found to hold only four slips of paper of the same general size as five-pound notes. Upon this discovery, he soon changed his tune, giving a full description of the man who had approached him near Sutton Coldfield with the sealed bag. "I knew he was a wrong 'un from the start," he whined, "but I needed the money. Business has been bad these past few months."

We left him in the police-station, giving what appeared to be a full family and business history for the past two years.

"I fear that the Countess' emeralds, for that is what I believe the bag to contain, are lost for ever," commented Holmes. "I hold out little hope for their recovery from the mud of the canal bed. And now, before we leave the fair town of Rugeley, we have one more duty to perform."

We bent our steps in the direction of the rectory one more time.

"I do not think that Mrs. Thornby will find herself seriously inconvenienced by our visit, despite the lateness of the hour," smiled Holmes.

We were received by Mrs. Thornby in the same room as

before, and Holmes explained the events of the evening, and the thoughts and deductions that had led up to them, which she received in silence.

At the end of it all, she leaped up abruptly, and exclaimed, smiling, " Then I am free of him ? The marriage was null and void ? "

" I believe so," said Holmes. " I think that no one could force you by law to remain in a relationship with that man."

She clapped her hands in an expression of pure delight. " Then you have done me a great service, Mr. Holmes. Not only have you set my mind at rest regarding the ghost that I believed I had seen, but you have released me from a bondage that I had come to detest." She suddenly assumed a graver aspect. " It is wicked of me, I know, but I cannot help feeling in some sense glad that Thomas Leighton has met his end."

" I cannot find it in me to altogether condemn your feelings," said Holmes. " But the greater villain who, I believe, is responsible for the death of the Reverend Thornby, is Brooks, whom we will quite possibly never see again."

There was silence in the room for a while, which I felt it incumbent upon me to break.

" What will you do now, Mrs. Thornby ? " I asked, curiously.

" Oh, do not call me by that name. It was never mine, I see now, and I am glad to revert to the name I had before I contracted that false marriage. I am now once again, from this day forward, Miss Anna Kingsland. And to answer your question, I shall return to my parents, who, I may add, were never approving of my union with— with that man."

" And I trust that this experience of matrimony will not

dissuade you from attempting the experiment in the future," I smiled.

" I make no promises in that regard," she said. " I must be content with what Chance will bring me."

" Come, Watson," said Holmes. " We must leave this good lady to herself. Madam," he addressed her directly, " I pray that all will proceed smoothly from now, but should you find yourself any difficulties vis-à-vis your marital situation, please do not hesitate to get in touch with me, and I will use what powers I have to expedite matters on your behalf."

" Thank you, Mr. Holmes," she answered him, taking his hand. " And thank you, Doctor Watson, for all your care and concern." Her small cool hand lay in mine for a moment, and I considered that it would be a lucky man who could persuade this woman into matrimony.

We left the rectory , and walked some half a mile in silence before Holmes spoke. " There is, I believe, a milk train which leaves here in the early morning and will allow us to arrive in Baker-street in time for one of Mrs. Hudson's excellent breakfasts. In the meantime, let us repair for the last time to the Talbot Inn, and refresh ourselves with a glass or two of that excellent Burton ale and whatever fare we can find there before taking ourselves to the station."

IF YOU ENJOYED THIS STORY…

LEASE consider writing a review on a Web site such as Amazon or Goodreads.

You may also enjoy some other adventures of Sherlock Holmes by Hugh Ashton, who has been described in *The District Messenger*, the newsletter of the Sherlock Holmes Society of London, as being " one of the best writers of new Sherlock Holmes stories, in both plotting and style".

Volumes published so far include :

Tales from the Deed Box of John H. Watson M.D.
More from the Deed Box of John H. Watson M.D.
Secrets from the Deed Box of John H. Watson M.D.
The Darlington Substitution (novel)
Notes from the Dispatch-Box of John H. Watson M.D.
Further Notes from the Dispatch-Box of John H. Watson M.D.
The Death of Cardinal Tosca (novel)
The Last Notes from the Dispatch-Box of John H. Watson, M.D.
The Trepoff Murder (ebook only)
1894
Without my Boswell
Some Singular Cases of Mr. Sherlock Holmes
The Lichfield Murder
The Adventure of Vanaprastha (ebook only)

There are also children's detective stories, with beautiful illustrations by Andy Boerger, the first of which was nominated for the prestigious Caldecott Prize :

Sherlock Ferret and the Missing Necklace
Sherlock Ferret and The Multiplying Masterpieces
Sherlock Ferret and The Poisoned Pond
Sherlock Ferret and the Phantom Photographer
The Adventures of Sherlock Ferret

Full details of all of these and many more at :
https://HughAshtonBooks.com

About the Author

Hugh Ashton was born in the United Kingdom, and moved to Japan in 1988, where he lived until his return to the UK in 2016.

He is best known for his Sherlock Holmes stories, which have been hailed as some of the most authentic pastiches on the market, and have received favourable reviews from Sherlockians and non-Sherlockians alike.

He has also published other work in a number of genres, including alternative history, historical science fiction, and thrillers, based in Japan, the USA and the UK

He currently lives in the historic city of Lichfield with his wife, Yoshiko.

His ramblings may be found on Facebook, Twitter, and in various other places on the Internet. He may be contacted at: author@HughAshtonBooks.com